60 Wei

Little Bluebirds, The.

StPatrick

4151

MW00768394

Acknowledgements

First of all I would like to thank God for my family, Jeff, Betsy, Cole and Joe, who allow Mom the freedom to be creative and for filling my life with laughter and love.

Next I would like to thank Nancy and Hamp Holcomb, for sharing the precious gift of their son, Jay Hatchett Holcomb with us all. In his brief life of fourteen years, Jay touched countless souls with a living message of faith, hope and love. Born with spina bifida, which paralyzed him from the chest down from birth, Jay was able to make us all forget his wheelchair and look deeply into our own lives as he and his family acted out the faith daily that they proclaimed. Nancy and Hamp magically taught Jay to look at his infirmity as a privileged assignment from God and to take every opportunity to share his faith. They also taught him what it meant to live a balanced life and to never allow trials to keep him from being thankful and having fun. Nancy and Hamp taught him this by practicing this before us all. From the moment Jay was born, they allowed us to hold him, to touch him, to play with him, to laugh with him and to love him. They allowed our children to do the same. At the risk of public perception, they transparently shared their struggles as well as their triumphs. By doing this, we were able to believe that their God was able to meet our needs as well. When I rushed to the hospital just moments after Jay was born, through her tears and a supernatural glow Nancy said, "Mel, you know, Mama and Granny always taught me that God's grace is sufficient...now I know it's true." The evidence of her faith continued to be modeled in the years to follow.

As you read through the pages of this book, with a child you love, you will see Jay's story unfolded as told through the legend of a little bluebird. It is only fitting that this family be portrayed as bluebirds, since they have brought such happiness and hope to us all. As this story touches your life, Jay's "assignment" and mission will continue.

I would also like to thank the following friends of Jay, who without their financial support, this book would still just be a vision.

Dr. David and Lynn Meyer
Financial Resource Management
The Twenty Group
The Le Bonheur Club

The Little Bluebird

By Melody Weintraub

© Copyright 2001
All rights reserved. No part of this book may be reproduced or utilized in any form or by any means,
including photocopying and recording, or by any information storage and retrieval system, without
permission in writing from the author.

ISBN# 0-9715494-0-0

The ways of the forest were quite different from the ways of the glen and of course, the ways of the city...that's in another book. In the forest, we cared for our own and we were always respectful of the ways of others. We built our nests quite differently according to the kind of bird we were, and the wisest of birds, if observing an unshakable nest in a storm, would have been even wiser to take note and adapt his own nest accordingly to make it stronger. You see, in the forest we learned from one another. That helped us survive.

For, although the forest was a lovely place, it could be a very, very perilous place. Sometimes, we were so taken by the beauty of the mist in the mornings and the way the brook rippled over the smooth stones, that we forgot the forest was not our real home. We would chirp and play and browse and busy ourselves sometimes as though the forest was all that mattered to us. Many of us would seem to forget that one day there would be a Great Migration from this forest to our real home. The forest was but a twig, a temporary perch. Sometimes, when we stayed perched too long in one place, we would need a gentle nudge.

One summer day was not unlike the next, unless the remarkable happened, which wasn't often in the forest. The forest was fairly predictable. Bear slept in the winter. Spring brought nests and eggs and babies. Summer was warm and green. Autumn was always messy, but colorful...and then it was winter again and Bear slept and so on and so on and so forth. However, the animal kingdom is still chirping about one remarkable summer day that changed the forest forever.

Deep in the Walnut Grove there was a tree that was ages old. Its roots grew deep into the soft, fertile earth and it was close enough to the stream that gives life so that it was constantly replenished. It was old, yet its branches remained strong. Many years ago, a family of birds decided to dwell in this tree. Many winds blew through the forest and storms would sway the branches, yet the nests remained secure and out of harms way for many, many years. These particular birds were called Bluebirds. They were a happy bunch, always singing and frolicking through the twigs, as though they had no care in the world. They went often to the stream that gives life and shared freely with other birds how cool they found its quenching waters.

The Dove visited their tree often and it was the Dove who taught them of the Great Migration. Many other birds visited their nests, and they mixed well with others, some who believed in the Great Migration and some who were just curious about the Bluebirds and how they lived. The curious would sometimes chatter among themselves that it was no wonder that the Bluebirds believed the Dove, for since He came to dwell with the Bluebirds, they'd known nothing but bliss. That of course, wasn't really true...it just seemed that way to the curious. It seemed that way, at least until one remarkable summer day.

The sun came up the usual way, streaming glory rays through the pine trees and making the dew sparkle like diamond dust across the mossy earth. The nightingale was asleep at last and the finches had begun their morning devotions, when the music of the morning mist was interrupted by a sudden commotion in the Bluebird tree on the branch where Mama and Papa Bluebird and their two babies were expecting a hatching. At first we all thought the family was just excitedly gathering around the branch to welcome the birth. However, news traveled fast through the breeze. A baby bluebird was born, but something seemed very, very different about the tiny baby bluebird...something even unpredictable. The Bluebirds were quite puzzled and called upon the wisest of birds, the Owl.

The wise old Owl peered across his foggy bifocals and said, "This is quite remarkable. I fear that Baby Bluebird has been born flightless."

"Are you sure?" Mama Bird asked. "Are you quite, quite sure?"

"Something must be done!" Papa Bird demanded. "Something must be done."

"Nothing can be done," Owl said sadly. Then Mama Bird began to weep. Papa Bird nudged her under her beak and said, "Leave everything to me, Mama. Baby Blue won't miss a thing."

Those days were quiet days in the Walnut Grove. The chirping was muffled, but the nest was strong, and Mama and Papa Bluebird learned how to take care of Baby Blue and how to take care of each other in those days. They stayed close and nudged much. And Spring predictably followed Winter that year and with Spring came yet another egg to the nest of Mama and Papa Bluebird. Now Mama and Papa had three strong babies to help them love and care for Baby Blue.

You might be wondering about the Dove and the talk of the Great Migration. Well, the Dove never left the tree from the time that Baby Blue was born, and Mama and Papa spoke often of the Great Migration to feathered friends and strangers alike...and even to the curious who came to see Baby Blue. The curious were also watching Mama and Papa Bluebird and the children and how they loved and cared for Baby Blue.

Papa fashioned a little splint for Baby Blue out of a toothpick and a paperclip (which is a people-thing that lawyers leave around in the grass on vacations) and a twist-tie that holds bread bags together. Papa had saved these for a fancy nest he was going to build one day until he got the idea for the splint. Mama was so proud of the splint and how Papa had thought of it that she showed all of her friends. Now her friends had babies too and many of their babies would ask why they didn't have a nice paper clip splint like Baby Blue, but they were told to quit whining. Many of the other baby birds wanted to play with the splint and with the tiny flightless bird, and so that is how Baby Blue became famous.

    Mama Bird had a lot more teas in those days, and mama birds would fly from all over the place to visit her nest. She liked that because she loved to sing about what she had learned from being Baby Blue's mama and what she had learned from the Dove, and since they were in her nest, they had to be polite and perch quietly. Mama Bird's teas were the most fun in the forest. She looked forward to the day when Baby Blue would be old enough to sing his own song. (Birds are not just about being able to fly, you know!)

Just when things were looking chirpier for the Bluebirds and they were getting used to the way things had turned out in their nest, Owl flew in to check on Baby Blue. Mama always got nervous when he came by...he never seemed to bring good news. He peered deeply at Baby Blue and lifted his wing to listen to his tiny heart. Then Owl shook his own brown feathers and turned his head all the way around without moving his body – which is a spooky thing Owl does sometimes-which disturbed Mama all the more, then he said, "Baby Blue has something very different with his throat and quite possibly his head. I'm afraid he most likely will not be able to chirp or even to laugh or even to make a sound when he cries."

Mama Bird wept again and Papa comforted her, thanked Owl for coming and politely showed him which branch to leave from.

"I can't believe it," cried Mama. "I wanted so much for Baby Blue to chirp his story and to sing of the Great Migration. Is that a selfish prayer, Papa?"

"There, there, Mama, don't cry. That's not selfish, that's just a mother's heart wanting to see Hope, but one can not see Hope until Hope is all that is left. Remember, I promised you that Baby Blue wouldn't miss a thing? Well, what is the greatest thing he is missing now?"

Mama thought for a long time, then she said, "Why, Papa, he cannot soar through the clouds and feel the breeze across his face. He cannot see how small the mountains look from above or perch on the Sycamore. He can't see the Trout swim in the river or watch the Otters play on Sunday afternoons. Papa, you are a good husband, you made a fine splint, you make sweet promises, but I fear Baby Blue is missing much because he can not fly."

"That settles it," decided Papa. "We need a vacation!"

"But how?" sniffed Mama, "we can't leave Baby Blue."

"Then he shall go with us! I shall fashion a way to carry Baby Blue on my back. And when we fly over the snow caps and rest in the Sycamore, he shall be with us. He won't miss a thing!"

Sitting high in the Bluebird's tree and listening intently, the Dove smiled.

Now Mama Bird loved to travel and see far off places. When she was a little peep, her whole family migrated to Africa for a season. When they returned they had many stories of their adventures, and Mama felt certain that one day she would return to build her nest there. However, seasons came and went and she courted Papa and they decided that maybe it be best to settle in the Walnut Grove, close to family and the stream that gives life and perhaps they could visit Africa on occasion. She often dreamed of Africa with its exotic beasts and beautiful flowers. She loved to visit with others who had been there and exchange stories and recipes with them.

Papa knew how much Mama loved to travel and Papa felt like it was his job to keep things as normal as possible in the nest, to keep Mama and the children happy, in spite of the extra-ordinary circumstances that had flown their way. So Papa began work on a new contraption to enable him to carry Baby Blue on his back as he flew. First Papa drew lots of pictures of this flying machine from different angles. Security and safety were foremost in his mind; however, Mama gently suggested that when the time came, wood from the Persimmon Tree might be pretty. Papa was glad that pretty things mattered to Mama, so he made the flying machine of Persimmon wood. The straps were made of the strongest cord Papa could find...a certain leather boot string. Papa had been saving it since he was a little peep in a secret hiding place. He had dreamed of making a tree swing for Mama, but even Mama – who knew nothing of his secret plans for the swing – would have agreed that Baby Blue's flying machine was much more important a thing to do with a leather string.

It took Papa all week to make the flying machine, and a week is like a thousand days in the forest. Every animal in the forest was buzzing about what Papa was doing and the curious came by often for tea and to take a peek in Papa's workshop.

When the day came for the Bluebirds' flight, every animal that was able stood at the roots of the Walnut Grove to see them take off. Hunting was called off that day, because Owl, who normally isn't very festive, declared it a forest holiday. Mama and the children helped strap Baby Blue to Papa's back and then she gently nudged him under his beak. Baby Blue's eyes were all aglow with wonder as Papa neared the end of the branch. Mama whispered a prayer and then with one big swoop, Papa leapt from the branch. At first the crowd of animals all gasped and then cheered as the air caught Papa's wings and he began to glide with graceful control toward the clouds. Mama was flying too just under Papa's tail feathers in the event he needed her support and the other siblings followed in order of age: Sister Bird, Big Brother Bird and lastly Little Brother Bird (who had to flap much to keep up!) As the Bluebirds soared over the sparkling falls, Baby Blue began to open his fearful eyes slightly and just in earshot of the crowd below, including Owl, he let out a miraculously loud, "Yippee!!!" to the amazement and happy tears of Papa and Mama.

That was the first time Baby Blue uttered a chirp, but not...definitely not. the last! He kept pointing out sights to his family as though they'd never seen them. And in many ways they hadn't really noticed a lot of things for a very long while. So Baby Blue helped them to notice more things. And when they safely returned home, all of their friends in the forest had decorated their nest with "Welcome Home" signs and such. The next morning, Baby

Blue started chirping about their trip to his friends and he didn't stop for two days. His chirping was music to Mama's ears. And she remembered Owl's prediction and Papa's promise. Friends would often tweet about how much Baby Blue loved to sing and what a clever way he had with words.

SPRING

SUMMER

FALL

WINTER

When Papa was at work, he would tell funny stories about things that Baby Blue had said. Papa's family was the delight of his life. Cheerful chirping had returned once again to the Walnut Grove.

Many seasons passed and Mama and Papa watched Baby Blue get older. They often wondered who would care for Baby Blue when they left the forest for their home in the clouds (should the Great Migration be delayed.) Sometimes they forgot the Dove would always be there and indeed it was He who helped them to think of ways to care for Baby Blue. Without the Dove, they would have wallowed in hopelessness. It was the Dove who led their family to settle in the Walnut Grove and to drink from the stream that gives life. It was the Dove who taught them of the Great Migration and Who opened the ears of the curious who came to visit the Bluebirds nest. And it was the Dove Who would care for Baby Blue.

Now it's a fact of the forest, that sometimes the thing a bird wishes for is not the thing a bird necessarily needs. Many times Mama wished Baby Blue could fly, when what he needed was for Papa to carry him so he could fly. Papa needed that too. However, Mama never ever wished that Baby Blue were a different baby. The longer he stayed in the nest and played in his little splint with his friends and siblings, the more she realized that she wouldn't change a thing that made Baby Blue himself. She knew in her heart that one day, he would be freed of all the encumbrances of forest life when he departed for his home in the clouds. She just assumed that might be on the Day of the Great Migration. So did we.

The Dove came for Baby Blue in the night. It was a gentle way to leave. The Dove swept Baby Blue into His wings and held him closely against the downed feathers of His breast. As soon as the Dove touched the Baby, he was instantly healed and he could fly at last and sing like a lark. As he set his sights for his home in the clouds, he never looked back at the snowcaps or the brook or the diamond mist in the forest, because they grew pale in comparison to what had awaited him. The only longing of his heart was to be joined by his family. The Dove assured him that that Day would come quickly, and he was comforted.

And quickly it did for Baby Blue, but not so quickly for Mama and Papa and Sister Bird and Big Brother and Little Brother and all the friends left behind in the forest. I know that is difficult to understand and even more difficult to explain, but in the forest time moves slower that it does above the clouds.

Mama and Papa awoke to find Baby Blue was gone. All of the forest was hushed. Papa, who always seemed to know what to do to fix things, felt stunned. Mama stayed very close to him. Feathered friends and the curious flocked to the Walnut Grove to be near their nest. It was very hard to see his nest and to realize that he was really gone. Some peeped when they looked at the encumbrances he had left behind. It was not the encumbrances that they loved so, or his feathers, it was something deep inside of Baby Blue. For some it was a mystery about him. Others who believed in the Great Migration knew that they would see him again. They wept because they longed for a certain Season when they would fly with him again and he would no longer need the flying machine that Papa had lovingly made. The curious began to notice how the Bluebirds took the loss of Baby Blue. Mama and Papa were not afraid to show their grief. The curious remembered watching them love and care for the tiny baby from day to day. The curious knew it was indeed not an easy life for Mama and Papa to carry, but the burden they now bore was much greater and caused Mama and Papa to fly daily to the stream that gives life.

This made the curious more interested in the power of this water and its healing effects. For, even though Mama and Papa didn't feel the healing right away, the fact that they visited the stream so often showed the curious the value of its sustenance to the Bluebirds. The Bluebirds were also unaware that the curious listened to their singing at the stream, and wondered how Mama and Papa could still chirp praises after all they had been through. That is how many of the curious became believers, but Mama and Papa would not find out for many seasons. For now was their time of mourning and in this time they felt a great void, so it helped to have friends, but everyone still missed Baby Blue and often chirped of him.

Mama began to look around at all the encumbrances that Baby had left behind. One by one, she began to give them away to friends who came to visit. Friends were honored and used them to strengthen their own nests. So, a little piece of Baby Blue's life was shared with others throughout the forest. When Mrs. Robin lovingly looked upon her powder blue eggs in the Spring, she saw beneath them a piece of persimmon wood which reminded her of the day Papa took flight with Baby Blue on his back. Mr. Bob White used the lawyer-thing-paperclip to sparkle-up the nest he built for his bride.

And with the leather boot string, Papa finally made a tree swing for him and Mama to sit in on cool summer evenings. They would perch and nudge and share memories of Baby Blue and the clever way he had with words and sometimes they would chirp and sometimes they would peep.

And that is exactly where they were when the Day of the Great Migration came just as the Dove had promised so many seasons ago. And those who had been curious and then believed were there. The old and the young, the exotic and the common birds were all caught up together in one Flock above the clouds, singing praises that made the heavens roar. And in the midst of the clouds under the wings of the Dove perched a tiny baby bluebird with his perfect little wings outstretched to welcome Mama and Papa and Sister and Big Brother and Little Brother. They sang and they sang and they sang and their tears were tears of joy, for they all forgot that they had ever been sad. The Dove, listening intently, smiled and the Bluebirds lived happily ever after.

The Beginning

LUKE:12:7

And he knows the number of hairs on your head! Never fear. you are more valuable to him than a whole flock of sparrows.